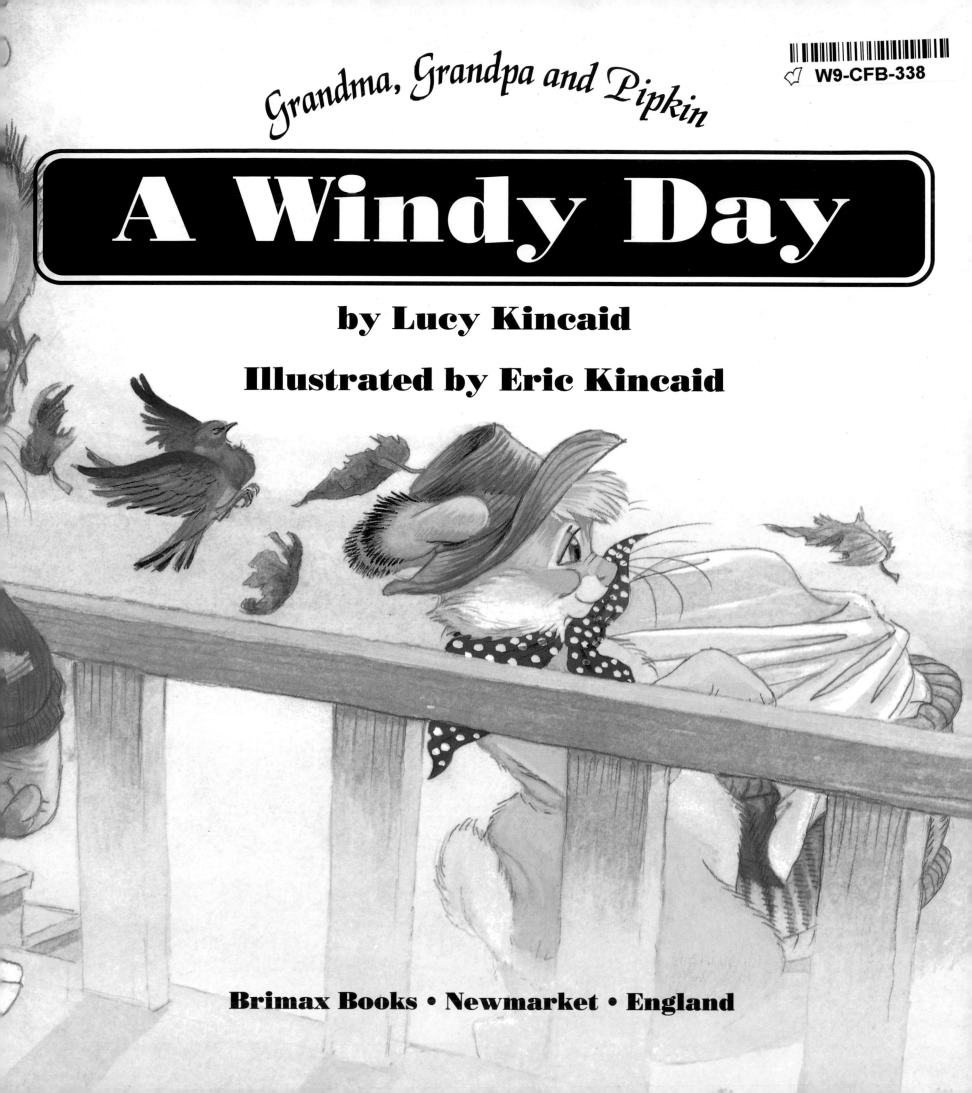

Grandma, Grandpa and Pipkin

A Windy Day

by Lucy Kincaid

Illustrated by Eric Kincaid

Brimax Books • Newmarket • England

It is a windy day. Grandma is washing
sheets. Pipkin is helping her.

"The wind will soon blow the sheets
dry," says Grandma.

Grandma is waiting for the next peg.
"Can you go a little faster?" she asks.

Grandma is called away. There are still
two sheets left to hang up. Pipkin has
an idea.

Pipkin asks Grandpa to help.
"This is not as easy as it looks,"
says Grandpa.

The wind is playing tricks. It is pulling at
the pegs. The pegs are getting loose.

The wind blows very hard.
The pegs fly into the air like birds.

Pipkin can see what is going to happen.
"Look out, Grandpa!" he shouts.
He is too late.

Before Grandpa can move, a flying
sheet wraps itself around him.
"Help!" shouts Grandpa.

The more Pipkin tries to untangle
Grandpa, the more tangled
Grandpa gets.

Grandma screams. She thinks Pipkin
is fighting with a ghost.

"Don't be afraid," says Pipkin.
"It's only Grandpa."
"Get me out of here!" shouts Grandpa.

Grandma takes charge.
"Keep still," she says to Grandpa.
"Unwind that way," she says to Pipkin.

"Are you all right?" asks Pipkin.
"I think so," says Grandpa.
Grandma takes the sheet to wash
it again.

"Look up there!" gasps Pipkin.
"What shall we do, Grandpa?"

Grandma will be cross if she sees
the sheet on the roof. They must do
something quickly.

"Hurry up!" whispers Pipkin.
"I am hurrying!" whispers Grandpa.
Grandpa has hidden the sheet.

Grandpa makes sure the sheet will not
blow away again. He pushes the pegs
down very hard.

The wind cannot pull the pegs off.
Grandma cannot pull the pegs off
either. Pipkin goes to get Grandpa.